Sacrament of the Forest
The Path of a Forest Mage

Totukani Amen II

Inner Alchemy's Publishing
Chicago, IL

Second Edition

ISBN 978 - 0 - 9961266 - 6 - 3

Published by
    Inner Alchemy's Publishing (Inner Alchemy's)
    332 S. Michigan Ave.
    Ste 1032 - C141
    Chicago, IL 60604 - 4434

info@inneralchemys.com
www.inneralchemys.com

Printed in the United States of America

CONTENTS

Chapter 1:   The Call..7

Chapter 2:   The Forest, its Spirits and
                  Animal - kind protectors.. 13

Chapter 3:   Preparation for the path
                  & Walking the Path.. 19

Chapter 4:   Emerging from Death
                  back into Life.. 27

Chapter 5:   F.A.Q..31

Chapter 1

The Call

The call of a Forest Mage is inherent and is part of them just as your blood flows through the rivers of your body. The calling typically starts at a younger age when the young child begins to want to hang out near or be in the presence of trees and the life that springs from these and the spirits that hang around that are unseen.

The child in question or even the adults that care - take for this human spirit may not understand why this is going on but this child is hearing the voice that now - a - days only few hear. Not necessarily because they can't, but mainly because they don't want to. They, meaning humanity can care less about the Forest that once covered the earth and the spirits that ruled therein, the spirits that gave man knowledge of wood, Animal - kind companions of life and the kindness from the agreement between the sun and earth to feed and care - take for human kind.

Because of life circumstances and the ever more steady growth of mega cities upon the earth and the poisons it brings, even less decide to take the calling any further than a brief thought or two. And while this brings sadness to those such as myself who have been granted with the secrets of the world and shown revelations of spirit in this time, it is even sadder how these forest are being utterly destroyed without consequence, its Animal - Kind protectors left without homes and the spirits that once governed them and brought fruit to man, left to only return to the Great Spirit Tree of Yah (Pronounced "Ah, or Awe").

In every age there has been that Mage of Forest who have protected it and made sure that it survives to nourish the earth for future generations but this time is not now.

The Calling is a journey in spirit but also a journey of flesh that will test the seeker in every way possible, to see without a shred of uncertainty

that the one who has heard the call is worthy of the task. That he or she is worthy to protect the physical representation of the spiritual forests of Yah.

For clarity sake when the Forest is spoken of this includes Jungles, Woods, Groves and the like. Each of these entities has a variety of Animal - Kind and spirits that govern and watch over it. And just as humans have distant cousins; so does the forest of the world.

Chapter 2

The Forest, its Spirits and Animal-kind protectors

E ach forest brings along its own set of Animal - Kind, and Spirits that govern it and no two forests are exactly alike. There are and will be similarities between forests that share the same geographical region and even those that share a continent together, but always respect each as its own entity with its own personality.

Just as human - kind has its own personality and temperament amongst each other, so does the forest, its spirits and Animal - Kind that dwell within its borders. Some Forests are kind and welcoming to those who wish to dwell within its sacred places while others are vile, ill - tempered and the moment you enter and venture deep enough you have sealed your own fate.

The forest, any forest, knows when you are near and is very much aware of your presence when you walk within its bosom. It is watching what you do, how you do it, your temperament, and your intended purpose if any.

The Animal - Kind that dwells within also knows of you and watches you from afar, sensing your energy and being if anything wary of you since it is your kind that is being the destroyer of the world. The archetypal, totemic species of Animal - Kind that you will find within are some form of Dog, Bear, Bird, Cat, Turtle and Beetle. Each serving a divine purpose within this sacred place, helping it prosper and if needed to defend this scared place, their home, to the death if required.

The Spirits are of many but I will give a few of the hierarchy within. First you have the Great Spirit that governs a particular forest; the larger the forest means usually it is older, and typically in which an older spirit governs it. The older the forest means the older the spirit and the Greater wisdoms that dwell within it that are shared with the Forest Mage of that realm. The larger forests that cover great areas have lesser governor spirits that help the Greater Spirit of the forest carry out its activities. Some

just as human - kind have an agenda of their own if the forest is not in harmony. Be aware and cautious of this fact when venturing deep within their walls.

Embarking on a journey such as this isn't for the faint of heart and many trying times lie ahead. But as such also many rewards are on the path for those who persevere through this difficulty.

I am not going to be coy in saying that most of you will make it. Most of you will not be found worthy to be the human guardian of the forest, given the title Forest Mage. But sometimes that is the purpose, for one to go on a path, giving their all for the sake of the journey.

As Master to those who find me as such, many blessings I give forth to you who read these words and wholly inner - stand that burning desire for the unknown and to know truth that dwells within.

Chapter 3

Preparation for the path & Walking the Path

The preparation for the path ahead is one of the most important steps for a successful journey. If you disregard this step or do not prepare properly there is absolutely no way to proceed successfully. I will not give specifics of forest to stay away from, nor of where exact vortexes to other worlds and openings to inner - realms within a forest lie. But what I will give is a manual that will allow you to proceed steadfast for the Great Spirit of the forest of Yah awaits your initiation.

First, one should pinpoint a forest that surrounds them that is no less than 3 miles diameter from center in every direction. This is the minimal size in which a spirit may govern. This does not guarantee that the spirit you seek is there and it also doesn't mean that this small forest was not, not too long ago part of a bigger forest. In which if the latter is the case you would need to look for the mother orchard since the one you may be looking at may be equivalent to one left to suffer alone.

Second, once you are sure you have picked the proper forest the next step is to not walk within its gates. You are building a relationship and as such must proceed slowly especially seeing the forest is naturally distrusting of human - kind. You shall walk on the out skirts of this forest, stating who you are, stating you have heard the call and that you want to share of its wisdom. At this point be quiet and listen for a sign of the forest to say if it will allow you to at least proceed within knowing your purpose.

Know that this walkin of its perimeter should happen at least 3 days a week, with a day between each visit, for a maximum of 3 months. At this period if you have not heard anything, and the silence is not due to your own insecurities nor lack of spiritual perception then either the forest you have entered does not accept you or there is no governing spirit within.

At this point do not give up, move on to the next forest and proceed to do the same.

Third, once you have been accepted to at least walk within its inner sanctum with it knowing your true purpose you are now able to start your inner transformation. You should research the forest in question in detail, knowing its fauna, Animal - Kind inhabitants and if able the history. As you are doing the aforementioned each day, up to 3 days a week with a break in - between you should stop by the forest in question and walk its perimeter stating again who you are, your purpose and then tell the forest of you, as you listen to it tell you about who it is.

At this point the physical transformation of you should start to take place. Ingesting internally only the roots, herbs, berries, leaves, bark, fruit and vegetables from the forest you wish to learn its wisdom from. Ideally directly from the forest in question if able but if not, buying locally from a farmer or grocer that serve the exact same specimens found in the aforementioned forest is okay. You shall not partake of any animal flesh of any kind of this forest or otherwise. You shall be just as the animal - kind and otherwise of this forest are internally.

If you were to dissect them you will notice the forest is inside them; and so shall this forest be inside you.

This transformation shall take place for a minimal of 12 solid months, which means four seasons have passed globally rather you are in an ever changing climate or not.

Your outwardly appearance shall take a more natural look for the parts seen and unseen. You shall be clean, and groomed but natural in all accord. No artificial dyes, artificial perfumes or otherwise shall be utilized during this time.

The mind shall be focused on meditation at all times available. And in visiting the forest as mentioned before you shall show the spirit of this forest via action, sincerity, and true intention who you sit on its perimeter, with a clear mind and listen to the wisdoms it wishes to share. This forest may be the equivalent of hundreds if not thousands of human years old of wisdom. It has seen civilizations come and go; it may have even experienced the Creator personified in the flesh walk with its bare feet through its inner sanctum, by blessing fueled steps taken step by step deeper within.

Because of this you show the up most respect, and as a student to teacher nothing is better than the enthusiasm to learn. What shall be shared with you is for you only and should not be shared with anyone under any circumstance. As the relationship builds between you and the forest spirit of Yah, this trust between flesh and spirit is one that men have longed to know, to experience and feel.

You have been chosen.

The above mentioned instructions shall carry on through the 12 month cycle and by the end of this you shall see a change in every aspect of your life.

This change can only be experienced and as such, I do not condone you to share.

A destiny has been foretold within these pages for those who wish to embark on a tale of spirit which few experience.

Chapter 4

Emerging from Death back into Life

N ow the time has come where the acceptance and the preparation to enter the sacred spaces of the forest now must commence. As you pierce its veil and move ever forward deeper into its embrace; you slowly unfold with each step revealing, unshielded your commitment to enter.

In every forest that houses a governing spirit; hidden deep within its bosom lays a patch of fungi or fruit like substance that grows nowhere else within its border. This substance is the forest equivalent of the semen from the male human - kind species and as semen brings further generations, this forest equivalent allows the spirit of the forest of Yah to enter within the physical temple. Beware that if a forest has many governing spirits than there would be this hidden patch for each one and if consumed would align you with that spirit governor and what it brings forth in wisdom. Ideally, if your goal is to become a Mage of the Forest you would only want to consume that of the Great Governing Spirit of that forest and no other.

The patch from the entrance into the veil to the finding of this hidden grove may be tiresome and you shall be tested through the journey within. On this journey you should not bring anything that brings offense to the spirits within such as a Gun. Ideally you should bring a knife for cutting food and firewood if need be, clothing, food substance that is found within the borders of this forest. If other items are needed but you are not sure if it would bring offense, please seek consul.

I cannot and will not go into every little detail of what one could expect on such a task either because it is for you to experience, or every detail illustrated here within this manual would make a bulky read which is truly unnecessary.

Once this area is found and you are certain it is of the spirit you wish to bring within yourself, consume as you will. It is best to find a comfortable spot to lie and I advise that adventuring at this point would be unwise.

Shortly you shall be overcome with the emotions of death, physically and spiritually and at this point wonderings of uncertainty and nervousness of if this path was actually for you shall invade your mind. But it is too late; this is the last phase of your initiation into the Great forest of Yah and depended on how great the spirit of the forest you consumed and how powerful its essence, you may surely die, permanently. This process of death may take hours or even days to be over and as this process is underway your body shall be looked over by the forest as she respects your commitment to her.

If you do not find the door way back to the land of the living and your physical body dies, it shall be memorialized within the forest by being consumed and internalized just as you did with it. If you shall walk through the door way back to the land of the living this means you have passed and yet survived this initiation and as such is one with the spirit you befriended all of this time. It shall now over time expose you to and trust you with the wisdoms of this world and as such, as the agreement you made, you shall protect this sacred place just as the Animal - Kind, Spirit - Kind and others protect it.

Protecting it with your life if necessary.

It shall provide to you what you need if you chose to dwell within its borders. And just as a child depends on its parents for help and to provide for its needs, so shall you help and provide for the needs of the forest.

Chapter 5

Frequently Asked Questions

1. Are you (the Author) a Mage? Are you a Forest Mage?

Yes.
No, I am a Mage of a different type.

2. How many different type of Mages are there?

There are a multitude of different Mages including but not limited to, Air, Earth, Water, Time and the list goes on.

3. Are there paths to different types of Mages? Will you teach these paths?

Yes.
I am not sure about the latter; some knowledge is not meant to be in the public domain of man. Not because man can't handle it, but more so because a certain type of man is amongst human - kind who only wishes to cause disruption. From this man certain knowledge is held.

4. To the Forest Spirits does it matter if I'm Black or White? Male or Female?

I will say the Forest of planet earth have a longer relationship with the darker melanin races of the earth, but just because you may not have much or any melanin does not mean you are automatically rejected.
Typically the role of bringing nourishment to the forest and helping with the overall flow within the inner sanctum was for the female species of human, while the protection and longevity of the forest was typically for the male species of human. But in these times these roles do mix.

5. Can I contact you for consul?

Yes.

6. As a Master to many, what would be your advice?

The road to higher spiritual knowledge does not reside within external things. It does matter not, how much material objects you can collect within a life nor what external God you chose to pray to. The path for higher spiritual attainment lies within the inner sanctum that is within you. This is the only place where the most private of lessons can be conducted that are then allowed to manifest into your external life.